Mysteries of the
Past and Present

商務印書館（香港）有限公司
http://www.commercialpress.com.hk

CENGAGE
Learning™

Australia • Brazil • Japan • Korea • Mexico • Singapore • Spain • United Kingdom • United States

Mysteries of the Past and Present 未解之謎

Main English text © 2010 Heinle, Cengage Learning
English footnotes © 2010 Heinle, Cengage Learning and The Commercial Press (H.K.) Ltd.
Chinese text © 2010 The Commercial Press (H.K.) Ltd.

香港特別版由Heinle, a part of Cengage Learning 及商務印書館（香港）有限公司聯合出版。
This special Hong Kong edition is co-published by Heinle, a part of Cengage Learning, and The
Commercial Press (H.K.) Ltd.

Director of Content Development:
Anita Raducanu
Series Editor: Rob Waring
Editorial Manager: Bryan Fletcher

Associate Development Editors:
Victoria Forrester, Catherine McCue
責任編輯：梁可茵

出版：

商務印書館（香港）有限公司
香港筲箕灣耀興道3號東滙廣場8樓

Cengage Learning
Units 808-810, 8th floor,
Tins Enterprises Centre,
777 Lai Chi Kok Road, Cheung Sha Wan,
Kowloon, Hong Kong

網址：http://www.commercialpress.com.hk

http://www.cengageasia.com

發 行：香港聯合書刊物流有限公司
香港新界大埔汀麗路36號中華商務
印刷大廈3字樓

印刷：中華商務彩色印刷有限公司
版次：2010年7月第1版第1次印刷

ISBN: 978-962-07-1911-0 (Commercial Press)
ISBN: 978-1-111-35146-5 (Cengage Learning)

出版説明

本館一向倡導優質閱讀，近年連續推出以"Q"為標誌的優質英語學習系列(*Quality English Learning*)，其中《Black Cat 優質英語階梯閱讀》，讀者反應令人鼓舞，先後共推出超過60本。

為進一步推動閱讀，本館引入Cengage 出版之*Footprint Library*，使用*National Geographic*的圖像及語料，編成百科英語階梯閱讀系列，有別於Black Cat 古典文學閱讀，透過現代真實題材，百科英語語境能幫助讀者認識今日的世界各事各物，擴闊視野，提高認識及表達英語的能力。

本系列屬non-fiction (非虛構故事類)讀本，結合閱讀、視像和聽力三種學習功能，是一套三合一多媒介讀本，每本書的英文文章以headwords寫成，headwords 選收自以下數據庫的語料：*Collins Cobuild The Bank of English*、*British National Corpus* 及 *BYU Corpus of American English* 等，並配上精彩照片，另加一張video/audio 兩用DVD。編排由淺入深，按級提升，只要讀者堅持學習，必能有效提高英語溝通能力。

商務印書館(香港)有限公司

編輯部

使用説明

百科英語階梯閱讀分六級，共十六本書，是彩色有影有聲書，每本有英語文章供閱讀，根據數據庫如 *Collins Cobuild The Bank of English*、*British National Corpus* 及 *BYU Corpus of American English* 選收常用字詞編寫，配彩色照片及一張video/audio兩用DVD，結合閱讀、聆聽、視像三種學習方式。

讀者可使用本書：

 學習新詞彙，並透過延伸閱讀(Expansion Reading)練習速讀技巧

 聆聽錄音提高聽力，模仿標準英語讀音

 看短片做練習，以提升綜合理解能力

Grammar Focus解釋語法重點，後附練習題，供讀者即時複習所學，書內其他練習題，有助讀者掌握學習技巧如 scanning, prediction, summarising, identifying the main idea

中英對照生詞表設於書後，既不影響讀者閱讀正文，又具備參考作用

Contents 目錄

出版說明

使用說明

Mysterious Crop Circles

Words to Know   2

After You Read   20

Expansion Reading: Crop Circles: Fact or Fiction?   22

The Lost Temples of the Maya

Words to Know   24

After You Read   50

Expansion Reading: The Maya View of the World   52

Mars on Earth

Words to Know   54

After You Read   80

Expansion Reading: Finding a New Home in Space   82

Grammar Focus and Practice 語法要點及練習   84

Video Practice 看短片做練習   88

Exit Test 升級測試   91

Key 答案   97

English - Chinese Vocabulary List 中英對照生詞表   99

The CD-ROM contains a video and full recording of the text
CD-ROM *包括短片和錄音*

Words to Know

This story is set in the United Kingdom. It takes place in the southern part of England.

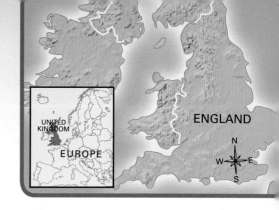

 Crop Circles. Read the paragraph. Then match each word or phrase with the correct definition.

Crop circles are large areas of flattened wheat or corn that mysteriously appear in fields of crops. This strange phenomenon has been found all over the world. Several of these unusual circles have even appeared in the landscapes of southern England. Many crop circle researchers say that the circles are created by people, but others believe that aliens make the formations. These people say that the circles are formed when strange beings come to Earth from outer space in their UFOs!

1. crops _____	**a.** plants grown by farmers for food
2. phenomenon _____	**b.** a living being from a planet other than Earth
3. landscape _____	**c.** the area where other planets and the stars are
4. alien _____	**d.** an unusual occurrence or happening
5. outer space _____	**e.** an area of countryside
6. UFO _____	**f.** an unidentified flying object often thought to be from another planet

A Crop Circle in a Field of Wheat

B **Other Mysterious Signs.** Read the paragraph and notice the words in **bold**. Then answer the questions.

Some people believe crop circles are messages from **extraterrestrials**. However, in the past, people on Earth have made some other interesting **signs** as well. In the English countryside, you can see **enormous** stones that are set carefully in circles, like the famous Stonehenge. You can also see amazing animal shapes that were **carved** out of hillsides long ago, such as the White Horses in the south of England.

1. Where do extraterrestrials come from? _____

2. What does the word 'sign' mean in this context? _____

3. What is another word for 'enormous'? _____

4. What is the definition of the verb 'carve'? _____

Stonehenge

A White Horse Carving on an English Hillside

Since the beginning of their existence, human beings have created signs on the landscapes in which they live. People from many cultures have long built unusual constructions, including different types of stone circles. In some places they have also carved animals, such as horses, into the hillsides. No one really knows why ancient civilisations originally made these structures and carvings. Some people suggest that different cultures may have constructed them as ways of communicating with aliens. Other people say that the ancient peoples must have created them to please the gods and keep them happy.

The country of England has a very long history, and its landscape has many of these old stone circles and carvings in hillsides. But in recent years, the beautiful **rolling**[1] countryside of southern England has experienced another unusual phenomenon – one which people all over the world have been studying with great interest. These strange signs have been appearing in local fields and are called 'crop circles'. The strange and mysterious circles are **puzzling**[2] to everyone, and have many people – even some scientists – asking: who or what could have made them?

---

[1]**rolling:** (esp. hills) gentle slopes that extend a long way into the distance
[2]**puzzling:** confusing; difficult to understand or solve

Did people enter the fields and create these crop circles? Were the circles made by aliens from outer space and sent as messages? The answers to these interesting questions vary and have resulted in a lot of debate among people who are interested in the topic. They have also resulted in a variety of theories about their origins.

Researcher Reg Presley has been **investigating**[1] crop circles for years. He thinks that most, but not all, crop circles have been created by people. He describes the beginning of his research into the phenomenon some years ago. 'I walked into the first crop circle in 1990,' he says, 'and I thought, "Hmm … I love puzzles." And what I did was say, "Right, I'm going to try and find out what this puzzle's all about."' And after all of Presley's studies, what is his **hypothesis**?[2] 'I think probably ninety-five percent of them are man-made,' he states. But what about the other five percent?

---

[1]**investigate:** to try to find out the facts about sth
[2]**hypothesis:** an idea that attempts to explain sth but has not yet been proved to be correct

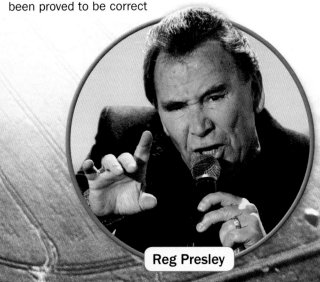

Reg Presley

Presley feels that some of the circles are so huge and complex that it's difficult to comprehend how people could have made them. He says, 'There's one [in particular] here, just over on the hill – Milk Hill – it's so enormous, that you can't even see the other side of the crop formation.' He then explains that the formation measures over a kilometre in width. Presley thinks that people couldn't have made such an enormous circle without other people knowing about it. At what time of day could the crop circle makers have created it without being seen? How could they have done it without leaving any evidence? Presley doesn't know, so for him it remains yet another mystery about crop circles.

Presley also points out that these kinds of formations appear not only in England, but all over the world. Similar circles can be found in a number of materials, from wheat, to trees, to ice. However, all of the worldwide appearances share one distinct characteristic: their **curious**[1] circular shape. Presley tells of a circle that was formed in a forested area near the city of Vancouver, Canada. In this arrangement, the trees were bent over and shaped in a circle. It is particularly remarkable due to the fact that, according to Presley, only the top two metres of the trees were bent. The trees were not broken suddenly and quickly as one would expect. Instead, they were bent over – without breaking – and arranged in the same circular spiral manner as the crop circles. Presley has also heard of ice circles, in which a circle of ice is missing from a body of water but the area around it remains frozen. Presley believes that a connection almost certainly exists between all of these mysterious circles.

---

[1]**curious:** unusual and interesting

Unexplained circular shapes have appeared in everything from forest tree tops to ice-covered lakes.

While Presley may have his beliefs about crop circles, others don't think crop circles are really all that mysterious. A young Englishman named Matthew doesn't feel that they are puzzling at all. Matthew is a crop circle maker, and he believes that the circles are always a form of art made by people. In the area near Matthew's home, many crop circles have recently appeared. While he will not admit to making any of these, Matthew has offered to **demonstrate**[1] exactly how crop circles are made. As he walks near one of the crop circle fields he says, 'Yeah, a lot of circles have been appearing in this area.' He then talks about how the fields look like blank artistic work space to him; a space that he wants to fill. 'It's a lovely landscape,' he says, 'and the fields are just clean and open like a **canvas**.'[2] As he gets his equipment ready for the demonstration, it becomes clear that Matthew is well aware of how crop circles are made.

---

[1]**demonstrate:** to show clearly that sth is true or that it exists
[2]**canvas:** the cloth on which an artist paints

Predict

Answer the questions. Then check your answers on pages 13 and 14.

1. What kind of equipment is used to make the crop circles?

2. What kinds of skills does it take to make crop circles?

3. What kinds of beliefs do people have about crop circles?

Matthew has his own opinions about the alien communication theories as well. He doesn't really believe the idea that the crop circles are aliens' attempts at communicating with Earth. Matthew actually finds the concept a bit amusing. 'Well, if there are aliens out there doing it,' he smiles, 'they're using **stomper boards**[1] and these little markers,' he says pointing to the tools in his hand. He then continues to explain why he feels this way, 'Because there [are] things there like **combing effects**,[2] which are people going around and around and around the same area, flattening it down.' Matthew then adds, 'That wouldn't be there with aliens I'm sure.'

In fact, Matthew thinks aliens would more likely use a faster, **instantaneous**[3] technique. He also thinks this kind of mysterious 'alien method' would be something that was obviously real to everyone – even him. Unfortunately for those who believe in crop circles, this kind of evidence is something that Matthew has never seen. The only crop circles that he has seen were undoubtedly made by human beings – and moreover, he knows how they were made.

---

[1]**stomper board:** a wooden board that crop circle makers use to flatten fields
[2]**combing effect:** the appearance that a crop has been laid down and shaped, as if styled with a hair comb
[3]**instantaneous:** sth which happens instantly; immediate

As Matthew and his team begin the long evening task of making a crop circle, Matthew talks about some of the beliefs regarding them. He explains that some people imagine seeing extraterrestrials, strange balls of light, or UFOs when they see a crop circle. Matthew, however, claims that crop circle design is actually a creative art form that is done by human artists. He and his team of two other young men have come to the field to show how it is done. They begin by walking around and around in various sectors of the field. As they go, they use their stomper boards to flatten the **grain**[1] into large shapes and patterns. It takes a long time, and a lot of work is required. As time passes and one sees the crop circle slowly take form, it's easy see that man-made crop circles are completely possible.

---

[1]**grain:** a long-stemmed food product used to make breads and cereals

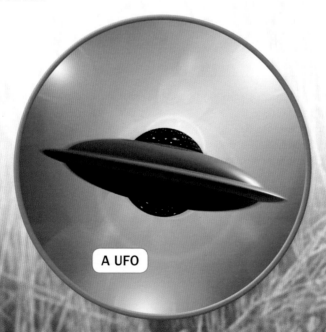

A UFO

Matthew then explains that crop circle design and creation often become a kind of competition. Teams of artists and designers sometimes challenge each other to see who can come up with the best designs. An enormous crop circle can have a huge impact on people. The designers also want to impress and amaze the public by showing what they can complete in an evening. That's the challenge of crop circle design, and that's also why it is so interesting and appealing to the designers.

Timing, however, is one of the biggest challenges for these crop circle artists. Designing and then making crop circles without being seen is very difficult; but, it's not impossible – and it's certainly not a mystery. Matthew explains how it's done. The basic principle is that teams have to work very quickly and efficiently. They must do so in order to avoid being caught and getting into trouble with the **authorities**.[1] As Matthew describes the process, it's obvious that it's exciting for him. 'It is a bit like a **military**[2] operation,' he explains. 'You've got to get in, do the job, get out, [and] not get caught, you know?' He then adds, 'It's **SAS**,[3] I suppose. **"Who dares wins"**.'[4]

---

[1]**the authorities:** the police or other official organisations with legal power to make people obey laws
[2]**military:** of or related to the armed forces of a country
[3]**SAS:** a part of the British Army called Special Air Services (SAS)
[4]**'Who dares wins':** an SAS saying that means you must be fearless to win

Excitement aside, Matthew does have some concerns about the crop circle phenomenon, but they're not about the people making them. Matthew is concerned about some of the people who think the alien theories are true. 'I'm a little bit worried about some of the beliefs I hear going around,' he reports. A wide range of theories are occasionally discussed in the media; some of them almost seem to have a religious element to them or even relate to the end of the world. 'Some of the stuff is a bit **apocalyptic**,'[1] Matthew reports. Another disturbing aspect is that some people try to influence others about crop circles and what they represent. They try to get other people to believe in, or follow, some very unusual theories.

These strange beliefs don't fool Matthew, of course. He has been researching, as well as designing and making, crop circles for a number of years. In all of that time, he insists that he's never seen any confirmation that aliens are making these mysterious, unexplained circles in the fields. He feels that the crop circles show signs of creative human beings, not extraterrestrials. In his opinion, crop circles are definitely not signs of intelligent life in outer space. However in some people's minds, opinions like Matthew's might be a sign of another kind of intelligent life – intelligent life on Earth!

---

[1] **apocalyptic:** about the end of the world

Infer Meaning

1. What does the writer mean by the last statement on page 18?

2. Do you think the writer believes that aliens have made crop circles? Why or why not?

19

After You Read

1. Reg Presley suggests that crop circles are created by:
   A. people
   B. aliens
   C. both people and aliens
   D. a mystery

2. According to today's researchers, which of the following is <u>not</u> a reason why ancient peoples may have created structures and carvings?
   A. to communicate with extraterrestrials
   B. for religious purposes
   C. to show respect for horses
   D. to show off their talent and skill

3. When Reg Presley says he loves puzzles, what does he mean?
   A. He wants to solve the crop circle mystery.
   B. He loves to play games.
   C. He doesn't know the answer.
   D. He thinks crop circles are difficult.

4. The writer does not suggest that Matthew believes aliens make crop circles.
   A. True
   B. False

5. In the first paragraph on page 13, in the phrase 'flattening it down', 'it' refers to:
   A. the stomper board
   B. the field
   C. the marker
   D. a UFO

6. In the second paragraph on page 13, the word 'undoubtedly' is closest in meaning to:
   A. imposing
   B. without question
   C. uncertainly
   D. consequently

7. On page 14, when Matthew uses the phrase 'imagine seeing' this suggests that he believes people:
   A. actually see aliens.
   B. pretend to see aliens.
   C. see evidence of aliens.
   D. perceive that they see aliens.

8. According to Matthew, what's one reason some artists create crop circles?
   A. to impress people
   B. to make puzzles for artists
   C. to trick other artists
   D. to show that artists can have fun

9. What do the letters 'SAS' stand for?
   A. Special Airforce Services
   B. Special Alien Services
   C. Special Air Searches
   D. Special Air Services

10. According to Matthew, why is making crop circles like a military operation?
   A. because it's serious
   B. because it's dangerous
   C. because it's secretive
   D. because it's apocalyptic

11. Matthew has never seen _____ that proves aliens make crop circles.
   A. many things
   B. nothing
   C. everything
   D. anything

12. The writer probably thinks that Matthew is:
   A. a smart man.
   B. wrong about crop circles.
   C. right about crop circles.
   D. a liar.

HEINLE Times

CROP CIRCLES: FACT OR FICTION?

The Heinle Times recently published an article about crop circles which brought interesting and varied responses from several readers. Here are two of these letters:

More info, please!

Your recent article on crop circles failed to include several important points. First of all, there was no mention of the huge volume of sightings over the past 50 years. According to one source, there have been over 10,000 documented reports of crop circles, as well as several other unofficial ones. You also failed to include statistics showing how widespread this phenomenon is. Crop circles have been documented in more than 29 countries – and that's just in the official reports!

In addition, observers at crop circle sites have noted that many of the plants are broken several inches above the ground, but the lower parts are not damaged. This simply wouldn't happen if people were using stomper boards. Also, soil taken from the inside of some crop circles indicates that it has been heated – possibly to as high as 1500° Celsius. I believe we need to take these findings – and their statistics – seriously if we are going to find out the truth about this amazing phenomenon.

Yours truly,
Richard Wellner

You've got to be kidding!

Your recent article on crop circles incorrectly gave the impression that crop circles are a valid scientific phenomenon! I think that this is a serious error in judgment on the part of this newspaper. Most people in the scientific community agree that crop circles are the work of humans who enjoy playing jokes on other people. They are not the result of visits by extraterrestrial beings!

Three years ago your newspaper featured an article about David Chorley and Douglas Bower. These two painters, who live in the English countryside, explained that they have been making crop circles together for years. They claim to be responsible for as many as 25 to 30 of them annually. I also recently discovered a website that describes exactly how to make crop circles. It has links with headings like 'tools' and 'techniques'. I feel that a responsible newspaper like the Heinle Times should not support the belief that aliens are responsible for crop circles.

'Most people in the scientific community agree that crop circles are the work of humans who enjoy playing jokes on other people.'

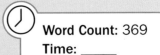

Sincerely,
Dr. Ralph Aker, Ph D.
Boston University

Word Count: 369
Time: _____

Words to Know

This story is set in Guatemala, a country in Central America. It takes place in a place where there was a city called El Mirador long, long ago.

 A **The Maya Civilisation.** Read the paragraph and look at the picture. Then match each word with the correct definition.

During the Classic Period from around A.D. 250 to A.D. 900, the ancient Maya civilisation was one of the greatest groups of people in the world. They built cities with thousands of buildings including pyramids for kings, and huts where poorer people lived. These pyramids were also used as temples where Maya people went to show respect to their gods. They were also places to bury the dead. After their deaths, Maya kings were usually placed in tombs within these pyramids.

1. civilisation _____	**a.** a small, simple building often made of wood
2. pyramid _____	**b.** to place a dead body underground
3. hut _____	**c.** a building where people go to pray to a god
4. temple _____	**d.** the culture and society of a group of people
5. bury _____	**e.** a special place where a dead person is put
6. tomb _____	**f.** a building with a square base and four triangular sides

a pyramid

An Ancient Maya City

a tomb

a hut

24

B) Digging into the Past. Read the paragraph. Then complete the definitions.

Archaeologists are scientists who study the past to discover new things about history. They often dig into the earth to find the ruins of ancient cultures. This story is about archaeologist Richard Hansen. Hansen is very interested in the pyramids of El Mirador which have been lost under the thick jungles of Guatemala. He thinks that the pyramids can tell him more about the Preclassic Period of the Maya.

1. The remains of very old buildings are also known as r_____.

2. To break up and move soil is to d_____.

3. A tropical forest in which trees and plants grow close together is a j_____.

4. A person who studies buildings, objects, and culture of ancient people is an a_____.

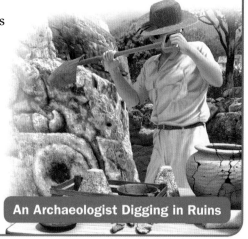

An Archaeologist Digging in Ruins

Preclassic	Classic	Postclassic

2,000 B.C.   A.D. 250   A.D. 900   A.D. 1,500

B.C. = time period before the birth of Jesus Christ*
A.D. = time period after the birth of Jesus Christ*
* in Christian calendar

Approximate Time Periods of the Maya

Archaeologists have been researching the Maya civilisation for a long time. Now, in the middle of the Central American country of Guatemala, archaeologists are finding new **evidence**[1] about the ancient Maya. They're discovering a Maya world that may have existed long before scientists thought it did. The secrets of this new discovery may lie under the leaves and earth of the Guatemalan jungle. They could be in or near one of the biggest pyramids ever built: the great pyramid of Danta.

Archaeologist Richard Hansen has travelled to the site of the pyramid. He suspects that the area around it, which is called the Mirador, may hold important **clues**.[2] By studying these clues, he may find information about the origins of one of the world's greatest civilisations. He thinks that they may **unlock**[3] the secrets of the early Maya.

---

[1]**evidence:** words or objects that support the truth
[2]**clue:** a sign or information that helps fix a problem or answer a question
[3]**unlock:** (literary use) to reveal

The culture that is thought of as the 'Classic Maya' grew across Central America between A.D. 250 and A.D. 900. However, archaeologists are now discovering a Maya civilisation that existed 1,000 years before the Classic Period. The Maya may have been a successful culture as early as the time referred to as the Preclassic Period. Most of the remains of this newly discovered culture lie under the ground in the Mirador region. They can be found near an ancient city that has been lost for hundreds of years: El Mirador.

Hansen has worked for more than 20 years at the lost city of El Mirador. During that time, he has been trying to understand the mystery of the early Maya. There are many questions to be answered. Who were they? How did they achieve so much? Hansen hopes to find the answers by digging under the pyramids. He hopes to find the tombs of the ancient kings of the early Maya.

Fact Check: True or False?

1. The Maya civilisation is over 1,000 years old.

2. The Preclassic Period comes after the Classic Maya Period.

3. The ruins of El Mirador are in the jungle.

4. Richard Hansen has been working in Guatemala for 30 years.

As Hansen explores the area around El Mirador, he decides to climb Danta. He talks about the huge pyramid as he climbs it. 'Well, this is the third level of the great pyramid of Danta at El Mirador, the largest pyramid at the site. It **sustains**[1] for nearly half a mile on **platforms**[2] below us here, and [it's] probably one of the largest pyramids in the world.'

The Danta pyramid was built during a time period that many people consider to be basic and simple. But if the early Maya were so simple, how did they build a structure that is as complex as the Great Pyramids of Egypt?

[1]**sustain:** (unusual use) go on; continue for a distance or period of time
[2]**platform:** a flat, raised structure

Danta Pyramid

platform

0.5 miles = 805 metres

El Mirador

The great pyramid of Danta at El Mirador is the largest pyramid at the archaeological site.

33

According to Hansen, things during the time period of the early Maya were not as simple as scientists once thought. He says that the kings of the early Maya civilisation were as important as the kings of the ancient Egyptian civilisation. 'The person that **commissioned**[1] this building was not a simple chief, living in a grass hut,' he explains, 'This was a king on the order of **Ramses and Cheops**.'[2]

---

[1]**commission:** to arrange for sb to do a piece of work
[2]**Ramses and Cheops:** two powerful ancient Egyptian kings

Infer Meaning

1. How does Hansen feel about the Maya kings?

2. What does the phrase 'on the order of' mean?

Some early Maya kings were as powerful as the ancient Egyptian kings.

Hansen dreams of finding these kings from the beginning of the Maya civilisation. He hopes that their tombs will show who they were. He's especially excited to find out more about them as individuals. Most archaeological discoveries focus on the physical evidence, or outer signs, of the power and influence of the kings. Hansen says that there's not a lot of knowledge about them as people. Hansen feels that the work that archaeologists are doing in Mirador may help scientists get to know the kings more personally. What were they like and how did they live? Their tombs in the pyramids may unlock these clues.

Stone from El Mirador Temple

Hansen is especially interested in one of the smaller pyramids of El Mirador. One of the stones in the pyramid has a large **jaguar paw**[1] with three **claws**[2] on it. Hansen believes that this could be the tomb of an important Maya king who ruled from 152 B.C. to 145 B.C. during the Preclassic Period. The king's name means 'Great Fiery Jaguar Paw'.

As Hansen **examines**[3] the stones of the pyramid, he talks about the discovery. 'This may be a **symbol**[4] of [the king],' says Hansen, 'that's why this building is so interesting to us, because it's possible this king could be buried here.'

---

[1]**jaguar paw:** the foot of a large, wild cat that lives in Central and South America
[2]**claw:** the sharp nail on the feet of some animals
[3]**examine:** to look at sth carefully
[4]**symbol:** a sign or object that is used to represent sth

jaguar

paw

claw

Is the 'Jaguar Paw' king buried in the temple? Hansen wants to find out. He has brought in a mapping expert and the newest technology in underground imaging systems. This special equipment sends electrical currents through the ground. These currents determine whether the ground is solid, or if there is an opening under it. The system then uses this information to create an image, or map, of what is under the soil. This map will show any open spaces in the parts of the pyramid that are underground. Will the imaging system show an empty room? If it does, this might be a place where Hansen could find the king's tomb. Hansen is very excited to get started!

The mapping expert prepares all of his equipment and sets up his computer. He then starts using the information from the equipment to create the map. After three hours, he calls Hansen over to his computer screen. He has a result. The system expert explains that there is an open space under the pyramid. The room, or chamber, is about 11 metres under the earth. It's approximately eight metres long by two metres wide. That's just the right size for a king's tomb!

Hansen may soon make a major archaeological discovery. They may have found the tomb of an early Maya king. How does he feel about it? 'It's exciting. Yeah, this is exciting,' he says with a big smile.

Hansen's team begins to dig. He is **determined**[1] to prove that 'Great Fiery Jaguar Paw' really existed all those years ago. The digging continues for some time. It's a challenging project as there's a lot of rock and earth to move. Hansen gives a report on their progress. 'We've gotten about 13.5 **yards**[2] into the building now,' he says, 'and that represents about 22 **cubic yards**[3] of rock that we've brought out of there.'

Hansen and his team dig deep into the Jaguar temple. Finally, they arrive at the place where the equipment showed a space – the room that might be the king's tomb. The team could be just a few minutes away from finding the tomb of the 'Great Fiery Jaguar Paw'. The team digs a short distance further. Then, they begin to pull away the last stones in front of the place where the opening is supposed to be. Everyone is very excited …

---

[1]**determined:** not willing to give up sth you have decided to do
[2]**yard:** 1 yard = 0.91 metres
[3]**cubic yard:** a unit of volume; a space that is 1 yard wide, 1 yard long, and 1 yard high

… but there is disappointment waiting on the other side of the wall. The room is not the tomb of the king. There is nothing behind the chamber wall when they break through. Hansen explains, 'There should have been a chamber or something there on the other side of this wall.'

How does Hansen feel about the unexpected result? 'This is a **setback**,'[1] he says unhappily, 'There should have been something there.' Hansen isn't completely disappointed though. He manages to come to a lighter conclusion about the kings who are so amazingly difficult to find. 'So, the fact that it's not there,' he says, 'tells us that the **elusive**[2] **Kan kings**[3] are still elusive.'

---

[1]**setback:** a problem that stops or undoes progress; a disappointment
[2]**elusive:** difficult to find
[3]**Kan kings:** a series of Maya kings from around 1000 B.C. to A.D. 300

Summarise

Imagine that you are a TV or newspaper reporter. Make a short report about the search for the tomb of 'Great Fiery Jaguar Paw'. Tell a partner about it or write about it in your notebook.

Does this mean that the mystery of the early Maya kings is just a story after all? Hansen doesn't think so. He still feels that they are real and he's not content to give up easily. The lost tombs are difficult to find, but that doesn't mean that they don't exist. Hansen is preparing to dig at another pyramid next year. Perhaps then this archaeologist will achieve his goal of seeing the tomb of an early Maya king. Maybe he will finally find what he is looking for in the lost temples of the Maya.

After You Read

1. Archaeologists found a big pyramid _____ a jungle in Guatemala.
   A. below
   B. at
   C. on
   D. above

2. On page 26, the word 'hold' can be replaced by:
   A. be
   B. reveal
   C. create
   D. cover

3. Which of the following is an appropriate heading for page 28?
   A. Maya Civilisation Is 1,000 Years Old
   B. Pre-classic Period Comes After Classic
   C. Early Maya Society and Culture Found
   D. Archaeologists Discover Modern Maya

4. What does the writer think the Danta shows us about the early Maya?
   A. that they enjoyed the jungle
   B. that they built a basic pyramid
   C. that they were not simple
   D. that they were basic

5. On page 37, who is 'he'?
   A. Ramses the king
   B. Hansen
   C. a Mayan chief
   D. an Egyptian leader

6. The jaguar paw symbol interests Hansen because:
   A. the pyramid might be the tomb of a famous king.
   B. he can use special equipment to dig up the earth.
   C. the stones show that there is a chamber inside.
   D. a claw symbol means there is an empty space below.

7. Special equipment can help discover _____ is inside the pyramid.
   A. that
   B. how
   C. what
   D. where

8. On page 40, 'it' in the phrase 'If it does' refers to the:
   A. imaging system
   B. king
   C. space
   D. map expert

9. On page 43, 'a result' can be replaced by:
   A. some news
   B. a decision
   C. a solution
   D. an idea

10. Hansen's team dug deep into the temple to try to find the king's chamber.
   A. True
   B. False

11. Which of the following is a good heading for page 48?
   A. Hidden Jaguar Paw Tomb Discovered
   B. Archaeologist Will Continue Hunt for Tomb
   C. Lost Tombs Do Not Exist
   D. No Chamber on Other Side of Wall

12. What is still part of the mystery of the Kan kings?
   A. the location of their tombs
   B. who the kings were personally
   C. if the kings existed or not
   D. all of the above

The Maya View
of the World

Much of the information that we have about the Maya was found in Maya ruins. The temples and pyramids that were built by ancient Maya kings are an important resource for scientists. By using information discovered in Mexican and Central American jungles, archaeologists have learned a great deal about Maya history and everyday life. They have discovered many interesting aspects of Maya culture which can tell us more about them.

The Maya people had an unusual and advanced numbering system. At the time, most of the world had no concept of the number zero. The Maya, however, were using a flat, round shape as a symbol to represent this amount. Their counting system had only three symbols: a dot, which represented one, a bar for five, and the round shape for zero. Certain numbers were considered extremely important by the Maya. For example, 20 was special because it equalled the number of fingers and toes that could be used for counting. The number 52 represented the number of years in a Maya century.

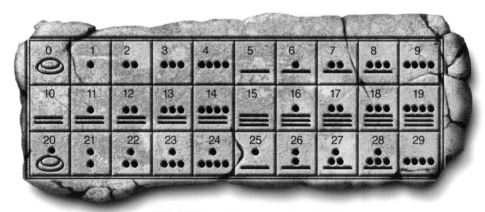

The Maya Numbering System

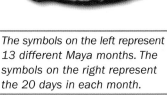

The symbols on the left represent 13 different Maya months. The symbols on the right represent the 20 days in each month.

The Maya calendar offers another surprising look at how they organised information differently from other cultures. They didn't use a chart with rows of numbers representing days and months. They used several different circular calendars at the same time. One calendar contained 13 months consisting of 20 days each for a total of 260 days. This calendar was used for religious purposes and for planting their fields. Another calendar had 365 days and was based on the movement of the planets. When the Maya referred to both calendars, they matched their 20-day months with the 365 days in the planetary calendar. When they did this, the days that were left over at the end of the year were considered very unlucky.

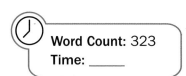

Word Count: 323
Time: _____

53

Words to Know

This story is set on Devon Island, in the Arctic region of Canada. It takes place in and around a large depression in the earth called the Haughton Crater.

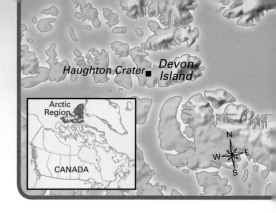

Haughton Crater ■ Devon Island

Arctic Region

CANADA

N W E S

A **Mars.** Read the paragraph. Then write each <u>underlined</u> word next to the correct definition.

Scientists and <u>astronauts</u> have long been interested in travelling to the planet Mars, but its extreme distance and <u>harsh</u> atmosphere have created a number of challenges. The surface is freezing cold and the <u>terrain</u> is covered with deep <u>craters</u> so it's difficult to land on its <u>rugged</u> surface. Moreover, the atmosphere is filled with poisonous <u>radiation</u> and dust storms often occur. These barriers notwithstanding, <u>NASA</u> or the National Aeronautics and Space Administration, anticipates having a person on Mars by 2037.

1. large holes in the ground: _____

2. sometimes harmful forms of heat, light, and energy: _____

3. the U.S. government agency in charge of space travel: _____

4. people who travel to and work in space: _____

5. difficult; hard: _____

6. the land or landscape of an area: _____

7. hilly; referring to land that is difficult to travel over: _____

Mars on Earth. Read the paragraph. Then match each word or phrase with the correct definition.

Scientist Pascal Lee and his team have come to Devon Island to field-test various equipment and device designs for future use on Mars. For example, they are trying out a 'thinking aeroplane' and a space suit that will allow space travellers to endure the difficult conditions on Mars. They are also testing a special type of greenhouse that could help grow plants on the planet. This testing is especially important in helping scientists develop robust equipment and systems that can handle the extreme conditions on Mars.

1. field-test _____	**a.** unlikely to need repair; tough
2. space suit _____	**b.** a uniform especially designed for space
3. greenhouse _____	**c.** test in a realistic situation or environment
4. robust _____	**d.** a building made of glass for growing plants

thinking aeroplane

greenhouse

The NASA-Haughton Mars Project

space suit

On the remote and **uninhabited**[1] island of Devon in the Canadian Arctic, day after day the characteristically freezing temperatures chill and the constant high winds blow across the **canyons**.[2] Despite the terrible weather conditions, which are to be expected this close to the North Pole, a group of explorers from NASA have set up a campsite in this harsh, unforgiving region. Tents and clotheslines full of drying towels dot the bare landscape. They belong to a group of people who are here for several months with the purpose of training and learning how to live and work on Mars, a planet that human beings have not yet been able to thoroughly explore. The group's members come from various backgrounds and nationalities, but they all share one common desire: to **formulate**[3] support systems for travel to Mars.

Part of the explorers' work on Devon Island will be to field-test equipment they hope will eventually be used on exploration trips to the distant planet. **In effect**,[4] they are preparing for the day that human beings will be able to land on Mars. To do so, they've come to this alien landscape to experience life in an environment similar to that of the fourth planet from our Sun.

---

[1]**uninhibated:** having no people living there
[2]**canyon:** a long, deep valley with very steep sides
[3]**formulate:** to develop a plan or system carefully
[4]**in effect:** in fact

The planet Mars has a harsh terrain full of canyons, valleys, and craters.

Mars, sometimes known as the Red Planet, is an **exceptionally**[1] harsh and **inhospitable**[2] place. The surface is freezing cold and the terrain is rough. At night, the surface temperature can drop to -73° Celsius and the atmosphere itself is poisonous for human beings to breathe. Add to those challenges the problems of radiation and dust storms and it becomes clear that surviving on Mars would be an impressive **feat**[3] of human intelligence and innovation.

Developing ways to overcome these challenges is what keeps researchers coming back to Devon Island each year. The rocky, treeless landscape of the island is actually a kind of 'Mars on Earth' – one that demonstrates conditions and terrains similar to those of the real planet.

---

[1]**exceptionally:** much more than usual
[2]**inhospitable:** unpleasant or difficult to visit or live in; unfriendly
[3]**feat:** an impressive act showing strength, courage, or unusual ability

Thirty-nine million years ago, Devon Island was hit by a large **meteorite**[1] that created a 20-kilometre-wide crater. Today, it's called the Haughton Crater and it almost exactly resembles the thousands of craters that cover the landscape of Mars. The similarity of terrain explains why training in the region makes perfect sense for scientists at NASA.

While it's safer and more realistically reached, Devon Island comes with its own set of dangers: unpredictable weather, high winds, and large **predators**,[2] such as polar bears, which may think human researchers could make a nice lunch! All of these conditions pose great threats, but despite the risks, project director and scientist Pascal Lec feels training here is **what's best for**[3] the team's mission. In his opinion, training in a place that is very similar to the realities of Mars is an excellent opportunity. 'By being faced with all the operational realities of having to explore a place for real,' he says, 'you are precisely building this experience to really plan an **expedition**[4] where all these elements cannot be left to chance. You have to plan it well.' That's why when Lee heard about Devon Island, he became convinced that it was the ideal place to train for Mars exploration.

---

[1]**meteorite:** a small body of matter from outer space that has landed on Earth
[2]**predator:** an animal that lives by killing and eating other animals
[3]**what's best for (sth):** the most suitable thing or option for sb or sth
[4]**expedition:** a long journey to explore a dangerous or distance place

Infer Meaning

1. What does the phrase 'operational realities' on page 60 mean? Look at the words around it and write a definition.

2. What does the phrase 'left to chance' on page 60 mean? Look at the words around it and write a definition.

When some people think of Mars, they think of astronauts in space suits. Here on Devon Island, Lee and his team are, in fact, field-testing the NASA Mars Concept Suit to see how it **withstands**[1] harsh conditions. Before it can be used in space, the **prototype**[2] must undergo heavy testing and be subject to qualitative research. NASA needs firm **empirical**[3] evidence that says the suit is safe in order to diminish concerns when using it in space.

The long testing process for the Mars equipment is not easy for the scientists and researchers involved. The suit is big, bulky and – according to people who've tried it – uncomfortable and **constricting**.[4] Simply getting into and out of it is a slow and difficult process, but walking around with all that bulk often proves to be even more exhausting. In addition, the scientists must spend hours out on the open lands of the Haughton Crater examining and refining the design of the suit.

It's not always easy having such an unusual job, either. At times some of the scientists and engineers can be reluctant to talk about their work. Why? It seems that people often simply don't believe what they do. Stanley Kusmider, one of the suit engineers explains: 'You're at the bar and you're talking to someone, and they ask you, "Oh, what do you do?" [and I say] "I work on space suits." [And] they say, "Oh ho ho! That's funny! [You're a] funny guy!"'

---

[1]**withstand:** to endure; bear
[2]**prototype:** the first form of an invention
[3]**empirical:** based on real experience or scientific experiments
[4]**constrict:** to become smaller and limit your actions

Depending on the perspective, designing a Mars space suit is either a great engineering challenge or a mechanical nightmare. Mars is incredibly dusty so the suit's outer surface will constantly be coated with a film of Mars' soil. This dust could **erode**[1] most normal materials, so the materials used to create the suit must be resistant enough to withstand its effects. In addition, Mars is exceptionally far away, so astronauts will need to spend at least a year using the same suits day after day. For that reason, the suits need to be extremely strong, reliable, and easily repaired in order to survive for the entire duration of the trip.

Kusmider's colleague, another space suit engineer named Addy Overbeeke, has spent his career working on space suits, and he loves the challenge of making one for use on Mars. 'You have to think about what they're really going to be operating in,' he explains. 'And [think] that "Hey, this isn't it. We have to make the systems more robust and we have to make the systems more **user friendly**[2] for them to operate in [an environment] that's even more severe than this."'

---

[1] **erode:** to gradually reduce the strength of sth
[2] **user friendly:** easy for people to use

The dust on Mars can be harmful to most materials.

Overcoming the severity of the atmospheric conditions on Mars is one complication astronauts face, but sustaining human life on Mars over a period of time is another issue altogether. It is a goal that raises a big question: can plants be grown in the harsh conditions of the Red Planet, thereby allowing food to be grown in order to sustain life?

Scientists believe that growing plants on Mars could be possible. Mars and Earth share many similarities. They both have about the same amount of dry land and have roughly a 24-hour day, which means that plants can **conceivably**[1] be grown on the planet. The experimental growing of plants on Mars cannot be conducted at this point, so Canadian scientist Alain Berinstein is attempting to grow them in the Mars-like conditions of Devon Island. He's doing this by working on a computer-controlled, year-round greenhouse that **simulates**[2] the scenario of growing plants on the Red Planet.

Berinstein explains how the greenhouse works: 'Outside the greenhouse, you can see that there is a **hybrid**[3] wind and solar power generation system that charges a bank of batteries, and now we [have] our own independent power system in place. And so now we are running in a totally **autonomous**[4] mode with our own power and communications system that will allow us to operate twenty-four hours a day, twelve months a year.' That means that the greenhouse can operate on self-generated electrical output even through the long, dark winter when nobody is living on Devon Island.

---

[1]**conceivably:** possibly
[2]**simulate:** to create sth that seems real but is not
[3]**hybrid:** a combination of two types of things
[4]**autonomous:** independently operated

In addition to the space suit and the year-round greenhouse, NASA and the researchers are also field-testing another new piece of equipment called the 'Thinking Mars Aeroplane'. Mars' atmosphere may be thin and poisonous to humans, however it's not too thin to fly in. Therefore, researchers have proposed using a robotic plane as a substitute explorer. This UAV, or unmanned aerial vehicle, serves as an advanced **scout**,[1] designed to search for and photograph areas of interest. But a pilot doesn't fly this plane, it thinks for itself.

Project contractor Greg Pisinich calls the device 'The Flying Graduate Student on Mars'. In his opinion, it is similar to these academic assistants at universities. 'You want something that has enough intelligence to make decisions, to look for the right science, to follow a hypothesis,' he explains. Just like a post-graduate student, who often does the **preliminary**[2] work for more experienced educators, the plane likewise acts as an independent assistant to the explorers. On Mars, it would do the preliminary mapping work for the astronauts so they would know where they're going when they reach an unknown area.

The images that the plane captures as it flies around Devon Island reveal an alien-looking landscape. And, while these test flights may seem like just for fun, they're actually serious research. The scientists are gaining insight as to how such a format could actually work once it's used on Mars. It's a step towards developing possible tools for future Mars explorers, and it's also a great tool for those working on Devon. The NASA-Haughton team often needs mapping assistance in order to reach remote areas of the crater.

---

[1]**scout:** a person or mechanical device that collects information
[2]**preliminary:** sth you do before an activity, as a form of preparation

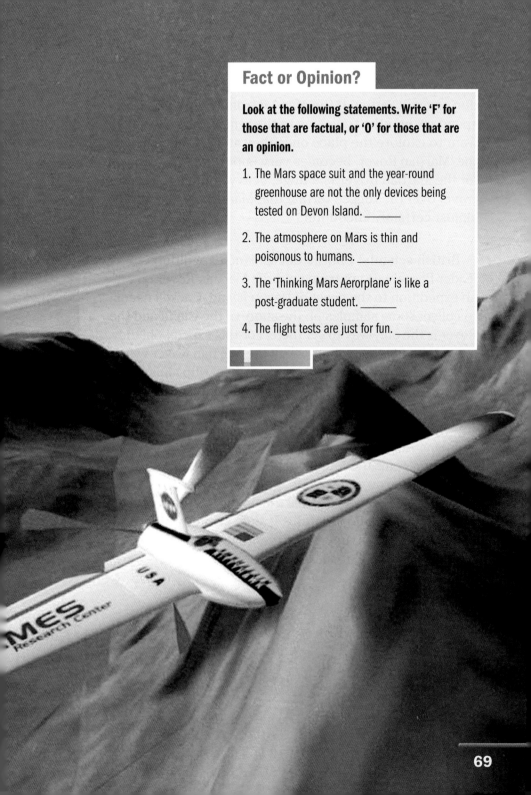

Fact or Opinion?

Look at the following statements. Write 'F' for those that are factual, or 'O' for those that are an opinion.

1. The Mars space suit and the year-round greenhouse are not the only devices being tested on Devon Island. _____

2. The atmosphere on Mars is thin and poisonous to humans. _____

3. The 'Thinking Mars Aerorplane' is like a post-graduate student. _____

4. The flight tests are just for fun. _____

The next invention being tested on Devon Island is designed to be a reliable form of transportation used during exploration. If the Mars astronauts are going to spend six months travelling to the remote planet, they'll want to explore the place once they arrive. That's when the 'Martian Rover' becomes very important. The concept for the Martian Rover is a huge, heavy vehicle that can travel over the rugged terrain that Mars explorers would almost certainly encounter.

British scientist Charlie Cockell and expedition leader Pascal Lee are trying out the Martian Rover on an expedition to the coast of Devon Island. Cockell needs to collect some samples on the shore of the island and the Rover is the only way to get there. For this expedition, they are combining the technology of the Martian Rover with that of the Thinking Mars Aeroplane. Lee, who aims to be the first person to land on Mars, wants to push the limits of the Martian Rover. He wants to find out how far they can travel with the help of the aerial photos taken from the Thinking Aeroplane. He looks at the images taken by the plane, and plans the route of the Martian Rover accordingly. 'So we'll head out from camp, go past the front of Marine Peak ...,' he explains to Cockell examining the transmissions from the aeroplane carefully. If they successfully reach their destination, they will have travelled further south than any previous Devon Island team.

the Martian Rover

an aerial photo of Devon Island

NASA's Bill Clancey has also joined the Rover expedition to the coast. He wants to learn how Lee and Cockell translate aerial photos into useful information to find the best route on the ground. Clancey explains what the information looks like, and is surprised at just how much Lee can understand from the images. 'It looks like a piece of paper that has gotten wet and it's been **crumpled up**[1] and it's just full of **wrinkles**,'[2] he comments. 'And Pascal looks at this [paper] and sees valleys, these valley networks, and he sees canyons, and he understands cliffs and **gullies**[3] here. It's remarkable.'

Lee, Clancy, and Cockell take off on their trip to the coast. As they travel, they seem to easily follow the route by using the photos sent from the aeroplane, which has travelled ahead. The result shows that the Martian Rover and the Thinking Mars Aeroplane are definitely **compatible**[4] systems. It still takes time for the team to find where they want to go, however, mainly because the distances are great and the Rover moves slowly. As they **creep**[5] along, Cockell jokes, 'Are we there yet? I want ice cream!' A team member then jokingly replies, 'Just ten more minutes!'

---

[1]**crumpled up:** sth that has been pressed into untidy folds
[2]**wrinkle:** a line or fold
[3]**gully:** a deep, narrow valley
[4]**compatible:** things that can exist together
[5]**creep:** to move slowly

The three men carry on with their journey to pick up the samples on the southern end of the island. They're making good progress towards the coastline and the Rover is doing extremely well, rolling along steadily over the difficult terrain. They've now travelled further south than any other Devon Island team. Never has the island looked so much like Mars. There are red hills and valleys as far as the eye can see. The landscape is empty and deserted, but nonetheless it has a strange beauty.

The team continues to make great progress, but then Steve Braham, a fellow research scientist who's working back at the camp, suddenly calls them on the long range radio. A huge storm is moving in, he tells them, and the team is in its path. Storms on Devon Island can be dangerous, so Steve gives them an order: Come home now!

The worsening of the weather conditions requires the travelling to cease and the men have no choice but to cancel the expedition for the day. As Lee and the other team members start their return to camp, the sky blackens dramatically and the wind blows fiercely. It's disappointing, but even though they didn't make it to the coast, they know that their expedition was a success. They have managed to test key systems: aerial photos, long-range radios, advance scouting techniques, and the Martian Rover itself. They had **anticipated**[1] some difficulties, but they are well aware that, in this harsh and remote location, simply returning to the starting point with everyone and everything safe makes the trip a success.

---

[1]**anticipate:** to think that sth will probably happen

The field testing on Devon Island has proved to be valuable and effective, but when will the researchers be able to actually build systems for the harsh conditions on Mars? The whole team is impatient to do what no human has ever done: land on the planet Mars. It seems like a distant dream, but NASA anticipates putting a person there by 2037, a relatively short time considering the amount of work that the goal involves.

There is no way of knowing if a Mars landing will happen any time soon, but suit engineer Addy Overbeeke believes that it's only a matter of time, and preparing for that day is crucial. His philosophy is that human beings were meant to explore beyond their present limits. 'We know that it's man's destiny to go out and do space exploration,' he declares. He then continues, 'It's always time to think about what you want to do in the future.' For these scientists, there's no better time than the present to begin preparing for their future, and they're doing it right here, their own version of 'Mars on Earth'.

Summarise

Answer the questions. Then write a report about this story or tell a friend about it. Use information from your answers.

1. Why did the scientists come to Devon Island?

2. What devices did they field-test?

3. Why was it important to test the equipment?

After You Read

1. According to the information on page 56, which of the following is true about Devon Island?
   A. The island is close to the North Pole.
   B. NASA scientists are ceasing their field tests there.
   C. Temperatures there are predictable.
   D. The soil there is identical to that on Mars.

2. The writer expresses the opinion that surviving on Mars would be an impressive feat because:
   A. other explorers have failed before.
   B. the conditions there are uninhabitable for humans.
   C. NASA said it was impossible.
   D. scientists can't even survive on Devon Island.

3. What does the writer imply about polar bears on page 60?
   A. They could be a danger to researchers.
   B. They like the same food as humans.
   C. The explorers don't need to be concerned about them.
   D. The explorers need special suits for protection from them.

4. Which word on page 63 is closest in meaning to 'observed'?
   A. harsh
   B. qualitative
   C. firm
   D. empirical

5. What does Addy Overbeeke mean when he says 'Hey, this isn't it,' on page 64?
   A. The space suit isn't good enough yet.
   B. The environment on Mars is too harsh.
   C. It's impossible to be certain about the space suit.
   D. His colleagues made a mistake.

6. Alain Berinstein's greenhouse operates _____ year round.
   A. one
   B. every
   C. all
   D. full

7. What is implied about post-graduate students on page 68?
   A. They are able to fly aeroplanes.
   B. They do a lot of preliminary preparation.
   C. They might get to travel in space.
   D. They are skilled at mapping.

8. What are Charlie Cockell and Pascal Lee using to guide their navigation in the Martian Rover?
   A. photographs
   B. an aeroplane
   C. plant and soil samples
   D. maps from great polar explorers

9. What does Bill Clancey find impressive on page 73?
   A. the aeroplane
   B. the information
   C. Pascal Lee's skills
   D. the valleys, canyons, and cliffs

10. Why do Lee and Cockell end their expedition early?
   A. They have an accident.
   B. There is a miscommunication with Braham.
   C. They have a disagreement with Clancey.
   D. There is a change in weather conditions.

11. Which word on page 78 can be replaced by 'critical'?
   A. valuable
   B. effective
   C. impatient
   D. crucial

12. What does the writer most likely think about human exploration on Mars?
   A. NASA won't be the first to send a team there.
   B. Exploring Mars is going to be an impossible feat.
   C. It may still be many years before it becomes a reality.
   D. It's too far beyond the limits of human beings.

Space Times

FINDING A NEW HOME IN SPACE

The dramatic rate at which Earth's population is increasing each year, the rapidly growing pace of environmental destruction, and the radical climate changes due to global warming all signal trouble for our planet. Certain regions of the earth may someday disappear under water and others may no longer be able to provide enough food to feed everyone. For these reasons and others, scientists have begun to explore the possibility of creating places for humans to live and work other than on Earth.

The Moon

In 2006, NASA announced plans to create a permanent settlement on the moon by 2024. This community will consist of groups of scientists who will take turns living on the moon for a few weeks at a time. Their job will be to explore the moon's surface and conduct experiments to determine what must be done to create suitable living conditions so humans might later live on the moon full-time. One goal of the programme is to find a way to create a moon community in which all the physical and psychological needs of humans can be met and in which they can eventually operate businesses that will supply products to Earth.

Comparing the Possibilities			
	On the Moon	On Mars	Space Stations
Travel Time	a few days	a few months	a few hours
Gravity	83.3% less than on Earth	62% less than on Earth	artificial gravity can be created
Water Supply	none	ice at the poles	must be created and recycled
Temperature	(lowest) -233°C (highest) +123°C	(lowest) -140°C (highest) +20°C	temperature can be controlled

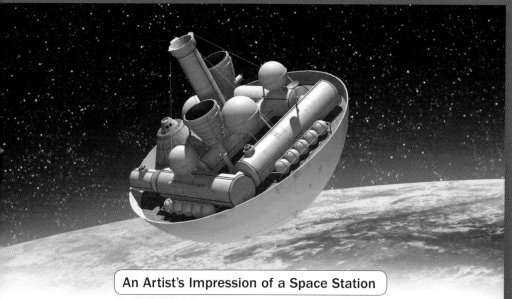

An Artist's Impression of a Space Station

Mars

Plans for creating settlements on the planet Mars are not as well developed as those for the moon. At this point, most researchers are focusing on the possibility that Mars might be a good next step, primarily because of its similarities to Earth. Unlike the moon, Mars appears to have water, although most of it seems to be frozen under the polar areas. On Mars, days and nights are approximately the same length as they are on Earth. Although temperatures are considerably colder than those on Earth, Mars is still the planet most comparable to Earth in our solar system.

Space Stations

Many people believe that space stations may prove to be the best way to create permanent, non-Earth homes for large human populations. Research in this area is focusing on how to make the most of building a settlement that doesn't have the limitations of a moon- or Mars-based programme. For example, Earth-like gravity can be created on a space station. The station can be located near Earth so that supplies can be moved back and forth quickly and inexpensively. Also, since a space station can receive sunlight 24 hours a day, such settlements would have a constant, plentiful supply of solar energy.

Word Count: 395
Time: _____

Grammar Focus: Perfect Modals for Probability

- You form perfect modals for probability by: *would/may/might/could (not)* + *have* + past participle.
- You can use perfect modals to express degrees of expectation or probability about something that happened. They often suggest an assumed outcome or an alternative outcome of an event in the past.
- You often contract *have* with *would*, *might*, and *could* (*would've, might've, could've*). *May* and *couldn't* cannot be contracted: ~~*may've, couldn't've*~~.

Certain:
He <u>would have won</u> the race, but he fell at the end.

Possible:
Her husband <u>may/might/could have taken</u> her car to work.

Impossible:
She <u>couldn't have driven</u> home. She doesn't have a car.

Grammar Practice: Perfect Modals for Probability

Rewrite each sentence below so that it expresses the degree of certainty given. Use perfect modals.

e.g. An animal made the crop circles. (possible)
  An animal could have made the crop circles.

1. Humans made all of the circles as a joke. (impossible)

  _____

2. Many people were curious when the first circles appeared. (certain)

  _____

3. Matthew refused to tell the reporter his last name. (possible)

  _____

Grammar Focus: Referring to Time in the Past

■ Time phrases can come before or after the main clause.
■ Use a past time phrase to show when the past event in the main clause happened.
■ Add a comma after the time phrase when it comes before the main clause.

Indicating a specific point in time in the past:
(amount of time) + *ago*:
Twenty years ago, we were a lot younger and less experienced.
in + (specific year) or *on* + (specific date):
Pedro started school in 1987. I think it was on October 3rd.
during + (specific point within a period of time):
We took swimming lessons during the first week of summer.

Referring to a period of time in the past:
for + (amount of time):
For two years, she didn't eat meat.
from + (specific time) *to* + (specific time):
I lived in Japan from 1994 to 2000.

Grammar Practice: Referring to Time in the Past

Fill in the blanks with the correct word in the box to complete the sentences. Use each word only once.

in	during	ago	from	to	~~for~~

e.g. She studied Italian in Rome _for_ three years.

1. The Maya kings were very powerful leaders _____ the period in which they lived.

2. The team dug _____ morning _____ night, but they found no evidence.

3. He often thought about a mistake that he made two years _____.

4. I saw the band's performance _____ 2003.

85

Grammar Focus: Referring to Past Events or Situations Continuing to the Present

■ *Since* can either be a preposition (*since 1998*), or it can introduce a time clause (*since I left Ethiopia*). Time clauses (subordinate) are usually in the past simple or present perfect tense. The main clause should be in the present perfect or present perfect continuous tense (*I have been to other African countries*).

■ *For* is a preposition that is followed by a noun phrase (*for over 50 years*).

Referring to events and situations in the past that continue into the present:

    since + (specific date or event):
        I haven't seen Mary <u>since 1998</u>.
        <u>Since I left Ethiopia</u>, I have been to other African countries.
    for + (amount of time) :
        She has been working for <u>over 50 years</u>.

Grammar Practice: Referring to Past Events or Situations Continuing to the Present

Write sentences about your life using *for* or *since*.

e.g. (more than five years)
    <u>*I've been studying English for more than five years.*</u>

1. (2005)

    _____

2. (less than two years)

    _____

3. (last year)

    _____

4. (my last birthday)

    _____

Grammar Focus: Negative Inversion

■ In a negative inversion, you always follow a negative adverb or adverbial phrase with an auxiliary verb and then the subject: *Never have I seen such a storm*. NOT ~~Never I have seen such a storm~~. Note that you need the auxiliary verb *do/does* even in an affirmative sentence.
■ You often use negative inversions to emphasise the point being made.
■ You use negative inversions more often in writing than in speaking.

Examples:
Rarely does James ask for help. (James rarely asks for help.)
Never had she been so embarrassed! (She had never been so embarrassed!)
Little did they know their life was about to change. (They didn't know their life was about to change.)
Under no circumstances will I go there again. (I will never go there again no matter what happens.)
Seldom can she take time to relax. (She can seldom take time to relax.)

Grammar Practice: Negative Inversion

Rewrite each sentence using negative inversions.

e.g. Ordinary people rarely spend time on Devon Island.
Rarely do ordinary people spend time on Devon Island.

1. The team had never experienced such a bad storm.

_____

2. The engineers seldom have a day off.

_____

3. She really does not want to live on Devon Island.

_____

Video Practice

A. Watch the video of *Mysterious Crop Circles* and write the vocabulary word you hear.

1. 'The beautiful rolling countryside of England has a long history. But in recent years, there's been a strange _____ here ...'
2. 'Some people suggest that different cultures may have constructed them as ways of communicating with _____.'
3. 'Did people create these crop circles or are they messages made by aliens from _____?'
4. '... Milk Hill – it's so enormous, that you can't even see the other side of the _____ formation.'
5. 'He feels that people couldn't have made such an _____ circle without other people knowing about it.'

B. Watch the video again and circle the correct preposition.

1. 'Yeah, a lot of circles have been appearing (around/in) this area.'
2. 'In fact, Matthew thinks aliens would more likely use a faster, instantaneous technique; something obviously real (to/for) everyone – even him.'
3. 'He explains how people imagine seeing extraterrestrials, strange balls (above/of) light, or UFOs when they see a crop circle.'
4. 'He also explains that teams sometimes challenge each other to amaze the public by showing what they can do (in/during) an evening.'
5. 'At times, Matthew is disturbed by some of the beliefs (of/about) crop circles.'

Video Practice

C. Watch the video of *The Lost Temples of the Maya* and write the word you hear.

1. '... the secrets of this new discovery may lie under one of the biggest _____ ever built ...'
2. 'They may be near an ancient city that has been lost for _____ of years: El Mirador.'
3. 'Who were they and how did they _____ so much?'
4. '... how did they build a structure that was as _____ as the Great Pyramids of Egypt?'

D. Watch the video again and circle the word you hear.

1. 'According to Hansen, the (queens/kings) of the Maya were as important as the ancient Egyptian kings.'
2. 'He hopes that their (homes/tombs) will reveal who they were.'
3. 'Hansen says that there's not a lot of knowledge about them as (people/rulers).'
4. 'Hansen is especially interested in one of the (bigger/smaller) pyramids of El Mirador.'

E. Watch the video again and circle the incorrect part of the statement. Then correct it.

1. 'It's approximately 8 metres long by 5 metres wide.'
   _____

2. 'We've gotten about 13.5 metres into the building now ...'
   _____

3. 'There's something behind the chamber wall.'
   _____

89

Video Practice

F. Watch the video of *Mars on Earth* and write the article you hear.

    1. 'Part of the work here will be to field-test equipment that they hope will eventually be used on exploration trips to _____ distant planet.'

    2. 'Mars, sometimes known as the Red Planet, is _____ harsh place.'

    3. 'When Lee heard about Devon Island, he was convinced that this was _____ ideal place to train.'

G. Watch the video again and underline the incorrect word. Write the correct one.

    1. 'And because Mars is so far away, explorers will need to spend at least a month using the same suits day after day.' _____

    2. 'Therefore, Canadian scientist Alain Berinstein is attempting to find plants in the Mars-like conditions of Devon.' _____

    3. 'This UAV, or unmanned aerial vehicle, is an advanced scout, designed to search for and record areas of interest.' _____

H. Watch the video again and circle the word you hear.

    1. 'Lee, who aims to be the first person to land on Mars, wants to (push/stretch) the limits of the Martian Rover.'

    2. 'NASA's Bill Clancey has come to learn how Lee and Cockell translate (aerial/air) photos into useful information to find the best route on the ground.'

    3. 'The field-testing on Devon Island proved (accurate/valuable) and effective ...'

(1) A young Englishman named Matthew is interested in the crop circle phenomenon, but as an artist rather than as a researcher. (2) Matthew is a crop circle maker, and he sees them as an important form of artistic expression, not as a mystery to be solved. (3) As he approaches a grassy area in the countryside, he says, 'It's a lovely landscape and the fields are just clean and open.' (4) Matthew gets a great deal of satisfaction out of creating complex and fascinating designs to transform open spaces like this into works of art for others to enjoy. (5) He disagrees with those who say that extraterrestrials are responsible for the many crop circles that appear worldwide each year. (6) He maintains that in all the years he's been creating and observing crop circles, he has never seen anything that would confirm the idea of extraterrestrial involvement. (7) In fact, he thinks that the strange ideas some people have about crop circles are a little bit scary. (8) He says that some crop circle theories have religious implications relating to the end of the world. (9) Matthew thinks that these beliefs are disturbing and that it is unfortunate that some people choose to believe them. (10) His explanation of crop circles is that they are a marvellous and unusual product of human creativity, not messages from outer space.

A. Read the paragraph and answer the questions.

1. Matthew thinks that _____.
   - **A.** people should not make crop circles
   - **B.** the idea of extraterrestrial involvement in crop circles is a comforting idea
   - **C.** crop circle makers are not artists
   - **D.** people should not attach religious significance to crop circles

2. Which of the following does <u>not</u> describe Matthew?
   - **A.** crop circle maker
   - **B.** researcher
   - **C.** artist
   - **D.** an Englishman

3. _____ is an unusual occurrence or happening.
   - **A.** A crop
   - **B.** Outer space
   - **C.** A landscape
   - **D.** A phenomenon

4. Matthew doesn't believe that extraterrestrials are responsible for crop circles because _____.
   A. he thinks they would make more complicated designs
   B. he has never seen any evidence that they are involved in making crop circles
   C. leading researchers have proved that crop circles are of human origin
   D. he has never seen an alien from outer space

5. Where should this sentence go? Although he has done some research, that is not his main focus.
   After sentence _____.

6. Which of the following flies through the air?
   A. a crop
   B. a UFO
   C. a sign
   D. a landscape

7. Matthew _____ a great many crop circles in his lifetime.
   A. must observe
   B. must have observe
   C. must have observed
   D. must observed

8. Which underlined word is incorrect?
   Matthew <u>may</u> have <u>learning</u> about how to <u>make</u> crop circles by <u>studying</u> existing examples.
   A. may
   B. learning
   C. make
   D. studying

B. Read the sentences. Write 'True' or 'False'. Refer to the paragraph if necessary.

9. The word 'them' in sentence 9 refers to beliefs. _____

10. A good heading for this paragraph is *A Scientist's View of Crop Circles*. _____

(1) The pyramids near the ancient city of El Mirador in Guatemala have shown archaeologists a lot about the civilisation of the Maya. **(2)** In this area lie the ruins of many important temples and tombs. **(3)** For years, archaeologists believed the Maya were relatively simple people. **(4)** Now they have learnt that the Maya had quite an advanced civilisation. **(5)** They find it as interesting as that of the ancient Egyptians. **(6)** Most of the current information about the Maya relates to the power and influence of their kings. **(7)** However, one archaeologist named Richard Hansen is interested in something else. **(8)** He wants to learn more about the private lives of the leaders of the Maya. **(9)** Hansen believes that the personal details will explain a lot about why the civilisation was so successful. **(10)** We need more scientists like Hansen who are able to look for answers to old questions in new places.

A. Read the paragraph and answer the questions.

11. El Mirador is _____.
    A. a large temple
    B. the name of an ancient civilisation
    C. the name of a small pyramid
    D. a city in Guatemala

12. What is the purpose of the paragraph?
    A. To compare the Maya with the Egyptians.
    B. To describe some important temples and tombs.
    C. To describe new discoveries about the Maya.
    D. To list some details about the private lives of the Maya.

13. The writer thinks that _____.
    A. Hansen should visit Egypt
    B. the Maya are more interesting than the Egyptians
    C. the Maya were not a simple civilisation
    D. Hansen should not study the private lives of the Maya kings

14. Where should this sentence go? Many are over 1,500 years old.
    A. after sentence 2
    B. after sentence 4
    C. after sentence 7
    D. after sentence 8

15. Which word means 'to place
    something underground'?
    A. tomb
    B. bury
    C. ruin
    D. dig

16. Which underlined word is
    incorrect?
    The 'Classic Maya' culture in
    Central America grew rapidly for
    A.D. 250 to A.D. 900.
    A. in
    B. grew
    C. for
    D. to

17. Choose the correct word to
    complete the sentence.
    The Maya built the first temples
    over 1,000 years _____.
    A. from
    B. for
    C. ago
    D. since

18. What do you call a tropical
    forest in which trees and
    plants grow close together?

    _____

B. Read the sentences. Write 'True' or 'False'. Refer to the paragraph if
   necessary.

19. The word 'it' in sentence 5 refers to the Maya civilisation. _____

20. Hansen wants to discover personal details of the kings' lives so that he
    can understand more about the success of the civilisation. _____

(1) As NASA plans future space expeditions, a large problem to be overcome is how the astronauts are to be fed on distant planets. **(2)** Because of the great time and distance involved, shipping food from Earth is not an option. **(3)** Therefore, scientists are trying to find a way of growing food under the extremely harsh conditions on Mars. **(4)** There are some similarities between the growing conditions on Mars and Earth. **(5)** They both have about the same amount of dry land and both have roughly a 24-hour day. **(6)** However, the atmosphere on Mars lacks oxygen while dust storms and high levels of harmful radiation present further problems. **(7)** So far, the best solution seems to be the use of computer-controlled greenhouses which can artificially create suitable growing conditions. **(8)** Initial designs include a wind- and solar-power generation system to support these food growing structures. **(9)** There will undoubtedly be more issues to address when such greenhouses are actually constructed on Mars. **(10)** However, the Devon Island greenhouse experiments are helping NASA discover possible ways to provide food for its astronauts on a long-term basis.

A. Read the paragraph and answer the questions.

21. Because the distances involved in space travel are so great, _____.
    A. astronauts must eat small amounts of food
    B. astronauts will never eat fresh food
    C. NASA is not able to send food from Earth
    D. NASA is studying ways of speeding up travel time so food can be sent to astronauts

22. In sentence 5, the word 'they' refers to _____.
    A. scientists
    B. growing conditions
    C. Mars and Earth
    D. similarities

23. According to the passage, growing food on Mars will be _____.
    A. easy
    B. complicated
    C. nearly impossible
    D. impractical

24. Because of dust storms and radiation on Mars, _____.
    A. the atmosphere lacks oxygen
    B. computers will control the greenhouses
    C. NASA plans to build solar generating systems
    D. plants must be grown in greenhouses

25. Forms of energy such as heat and light are called _____.
    A. greenhouse
    B. radiation
    C. crater
    D. astronaut

26. Which underlined group of words is incorrect?
    <u>Never I will</u> <u>understand how</u> astronauts <u>are able to</u> spend months without <u>taking off</u> their space suits.
    A. Never I will
    B. understand how
    C. are able to
    D. taking off

27. _____ do researchers fail to find a solution to a problem.
    A. Sometimes
    B. Rarely
    C. Occasionally
    D. Usually

28. Where should this sentence go?
    The energy generated allows the greenhouses to operate 24 hours a day.
    After sentence _____.

B. Read the sentences. Write 'True' or 'False'. Refer to the paragraph if necessary.

29. There is much less harmful radiation on Mars than on Earth. _____

30. Explorers on Mars will need special space suits to protect them from the harsh environment. _____

Key 答案

Mysterious Crop Circles

Words to Know: A. 1. a **2.** d **3.** e **4.** b **5.** c **6.** f **B.** (suggested answers)
1. a planet other than Earth; outer space **2.** a construction **3.** very large
4. to cut a pattern on the surface of something

Predict: (suggested answers) **1.** stomper boards and markers **2.** creative
skill and the ability to work hard **3.** Some people imagine seeing
extraterrestrials, strange balls of light, or UFOs when they see a crop
circle.

Infer Meaning: (suggested answers) **1.** Matthew's ideas sound the most
reasonable. **2.** No, because the writer refers to Matthew's opinions as
proof of intelligent life on Earth.

After You Read: 1. C **2.** D **3.** A **4.** A **5.** B **6.** B **7.** D **8.** A **9.** D **10.** C **11.** D
12. C

The Lost Temples of the Maya

Words to Know: A. 1. d **2.** f **3.** a **4.** c **5.** b **6.** e **B. 1.** ruins **2.** dig
3. jungle **4.** archaeologist

Fact Check: True or False?: 1. T **2.** F **3.** T **4.** F

Infer Meaning: (suggested answers) **1.** He is greatly impressed by them.
2. similar to, like, at the same level as

Summarise: (suggested answers) In the jungles of Guatemala,
archaeologists thought they were about to discover the tomb of a lost
Maya king today. They used the newest technology to find the spot, but
after digging excitedly, they found nothing. Unfortunately, today brings
no answers, only more questions, about these ancient leaders.

After You Read: 1. A **2.** B **3.** C **4.** C **5.** B **6.** A **7.** C **8.** A **9.** A **10.** A
11. B **12.** D

Mars on Earth

Words to Know: A. 1. craters **2.** radiation **3.** NASA **4.** astronauts
5. harsh **6.** terrain **7.** rugged **B. 1.** c **2.** b **3.** d **4.** a

Infer Meaning: (suggested answers) **1.** the actual circumstances and
practices of a place/situation **2.** out of human control

Fact or Opinion?: 1. F **2.** F **3.** O **4.** O

Summarise: (suggested answers) **1.** to test equipment to use on Mars
2. space suits, greenhouse, aeroplane, vehicle **3.** to make sure the
equipment works before using it on Mars

After You Read: 1. A **2.** B **3.** A **4.** D **5.** A **6.** C **7.** B **8.** A **9.** C **10.** D
11. D **12.** C

Grammar Practice

Perfect Modals for Probability: 1. Humans couldn't have made all of the circles as a joke. **2.** Many people would have been curious when the first circles appeared. **3.** Matthew may/might/could have refused to tell the reporter his last name.

Referring to Time in the Past: 1. during **2.** from, to **3.** ago **4.** in

Referring to Past Events or Situations Continuing to the Present: open answers

Negative Inversion: 1. Never had the team experienced such a bad storm. **2.** Seldom do the engineers have a day off. **3.** Under no circumstances will she live on Devon Island.

Video Practice

A. 1. phenomenon **2.** aliens **3.** outer space **4.** crop **5.** enormous **B. 1.** in **2.** to **3.** of **4.** in **5.** about **C. 1.** pyramids **2.** hundreds **3.** achieve **4.** complex **D. 1.** kings **2.** tombs **3.** people **4.** smaller **E. 1.** 5 (2) **2.** metres (yards) **3.** something (nothing) **F. 1.** the **2.** a **3.** the **G. 1.** month (year) **2.** find (grow) **3.** record (photograph) **H. 1.** push **2.** aerial **3.** valuable

Exit Test

1. D **2.** B **3.** D **4.** B **5.** 1 **6.** B **7.** C **8.** B **9.** T **10.** F **11.** D **12.** C **13.** C **14.** A **15.** B **16.** C **17.** C **18.** a jungle **19.** T **20.** T **21.** C **22.** C **23.** B **24.** D **25.** B **26.** A **27.** B **28.** 8 **29.** F **30.** T

English - Chinese Vocabulary List 中英對照生詞表

(Arranged in alphabetical order)

English	Chinese	English	Chinese
anticipate	預計	**feat**	功績
apocalyptic	預言世界末日的	**formulate**	制定
autonomous	自主的	**grain**	穀物
canvas	油畫布	**gully**	峽谷
canyon	峽谷	**hybrid**	混合物
claw	爪	**hypothesis**	假設
clue	提示	**in effect**	事實上
combing effect	梳理作用	**inhospitable**	不適宜居住的
commission	委託	**instantaneous**	瞬間的
compatible	能共存的	**investigate**	調查
conceivably	可能	**jaguar paw**	美洲豹的腳掌
constrict	使收縮	**Kan kings**	瑪雅皇帝
creep	緩慢地走	**meteorite**	隕石
crumple up	弄皺/揉成一團	**military**	軍隊的
cubic yard	立方碼	**platform**	高台
curious	奇特的	**predator**	肉食動物
demonstrate	證明	**preliminary**	初步的/預備性的
determined	堅定不移的	**prototype**	原型/樣品
elusive	難找到的	**puzzling**	令人困惑的
empirical	以經驗或實驗為根據的	**Ramses and Cheops**	拉美西斯與齊阿普斯
erode	(逐步)削弱	**rolling**	延綿起伏的
evidence	證據	**SAS**	英國皇家空軍特種部隊
examine	仔細檢查	**scout**	偵察員/機
exceptionally	格外地	**setback**	障礙/挫折
expedition	考察	**simulate**	模擬

stomper board	用以製造麥田圈的木板	**user friendly**	容易使用的
sustain	維持	**what's best for (sth)**	對...最好的事
symbol	象徵/標誌	**'Who dares wins'**	勇者為勝
the authorities	當局	**withstand**	承受住/抵擋
uninhabited	無人居住的	**wrinkle**	皺紋
unlock	揭開	**yard**	碼